Mystery Cove

Cathy MacPhail ▪ David Belmonte

OXFORD
UNIVERSITY PRESS

Chapter 1

There was something in the dark, watching
her, waiting for her. It had green slits for
eyes; they gleamed in the black night. Becca
drew in her breath, ready to scream but a
scream wouldn't come. The thing moved,
a scaly tail flicked, the green eyes blinked.
Becca tried to scramble back but she was too
afraid to move. The thing stayed as still as a
gargoyle, the green eyes never leaving her.
She knew that at any second it would leap
towards her. She had to run. She had to get
away. If she didn't, this green-eyed, menacing
creature would soon be upon her.

Becca's eyes snapped open. She was bathed in sweat and her heart was beating rapidly. It had only been the nightmare, always the same one – the green-eyed monster staring at her out of the darkness. She breathed a long sigh of relief. It was only a dream. She was safe.

The morning sun streaked through a gap in the curtains and she could hear her mum rustling about in the kitchen, packing up everything for their holiday. She wouldn't tell Mum about the nightmare. Not this time. It would only worry her, as she thought Becca had bad dreams because she was missing Dad. Maybe her mum was right: she missed him every single day. Becca pushed those thoughts aside. She was awake now and tonight she'd be sleeping in their holiday house by the sea. The one they rented every year.

She wouldn't have any nightmares there.

The wind buffeted Becca and her mum as they arrived at the house. Even the seagulls seemed to be struggling to stay aloft as they circled in the air high above them.

"Going to rain later," Mr Tavish, the caretaker, said. Becca remembered him from last year. He was a wiry man with a long, thin face and a thatch of white hair that made him look older than he probably was. "And how have you been, Becca?"

It was her mum who answered. "She's fine. She's going to be extra careful this year, aren't you, Becca?"

Mr Tavish bared his teeth in a smile. *A skeleton's smile*, Becca thought with a shiver. "Yes, you were wrapped up like a mummy by the time you left last year, weren't you?"

That's a bit of an exaggeration, Becca thought. Would they ever let her forget it? How stupid she'd been, running into a pile of deckchairs and later slipping on the rocks. She was normally really careful but anyone can have an accident, can't they? There's nothing strange about that.

After Mr Tavish left, Lena, the woman who lived in the house next door, arrived with a welcome pack for them: milk, bread, butter and eggs. Lena had stylish blonde hair, polished nails and a crystal-white smile. She was a real businesswoman, too, and owned several of the holiday houses in the town. Becca was glad her mum got on well with Lena, especially now that Dad was gone; it was good for her to have a friend here.

"Can I go out, Mum?" she asked.

It was Lena who answered her. "Don't go far, will you? Oh, and be careful."

As if it's her place to say that, Becca thought crossly. It seemed no one trusted her any more – at least, not since the accident. Becca held out her mobile phone, which her mum insisted she have with her at all times. "I'll keep in touch, don't worry," replied Becca as she stormed off.

9

Chapter 2

Becca wandered down towards the sea. It was a shingly beach, filled with shells and rocks, but Becca loved it. The cries of the seagulls filled the threatening sky. White waves crashed against the rocks and Becca could taste the salty air on her lips. It was so windy she hugged her jacket tight around her and pulled her collar up, nestling into it for warmth.

She was all alone, the other holidaymakers preferred the sandy beach and sheltered coves on the other side of the bay. She made her way to her favourite spot. Here, in a little nook in the rocks, she was sheltered from the wind but had a spectacular view of the bay.

The sounds and the smells surrounded her like a thick, comforting blanket. She felt safe here. This was her secret place, though she often wondered if anyone else had discovered this perfect little spot. She hated the idea that someone else might have found it, too. This was *her* sanctuary!

She leaned back and closed her eyes but she couldn't get comfortable: something was digging into her back. She turned and saw a little edge of plastic jammed between the rocks, almost hidden – almost, but not quite. She peered closer: there was something inside the plastic, a notebook of some kind. *Funny thing to be hidden away in such a place*, she thought.

Becca couldn't resist. She tugged the bag free. A small notebook with a hard blue cover was sealed inside.

Becca stood up and looked around, half expecting to see someone running across the rocks, yelling at her to leave their notebook alone. But there was no one on the beach. All she could see was a small boat in the distance, bobbing up and down.

Becca sat down again and slipped the notebook out of the bag. There was no name on the front. Nothing said: 'This notebook belongs to ...' or 'Private! Keep out!'.

After a moment's hesitation, she opened the little blue book and began to read. *What terrible handwriting*, she thought. It reminded her of someone. Her cousin, Josh, probably – his scribbles looked a lot like this.

Monday 8th July

I sit here and watch every day and I see strange things. Things I don't understand; so I'm going to keep a record in this diary of everything I see.

So it was a diary. Becca closed it. She knew deep down she shouldn't be reading someone else's private thoughts; someone who, like her, came here every day, probably searching for some privacy.

Could it be someone who's on holiday now, staying in one of the other holiday houses? Someone who thinks they've discovered a mystery? Maybe someone like Josh who looks for mysteries everywhere: mysterious disappearances, dead bodies hidden in the boiler room...

Well, she wouldn't read any more. It was none of her business. She put the diary back inside the plastic bag and pushed it carefully into the crack in the rocks. She had to admit that whoever it was had found a perfect place to hide their secrets, tucked away from the world.

Becca's phone rang and she jumped guiltily. For a second she thought that it might be the diary's owner – that they'd been hidden from view somewhere on the beach and had spotted her with the diary! Silly, of course.

It was her mum. "Time to come home, Becca."

She began to clamber back over the rocks. This mystery would have to wait.

Chapter 3

"We're going to a barbecue tomorrow," her mum said later that evening. "It's at Lena's and she's invited all the people in the holiday houses, apparently. You might make some friends."

Her mother added that last part hopefully. She worried that Becca was always alone but being alone didn't bother Becca. *The barbecue might prove useful though,* she thought. *The author of the diary might be there.*

The next day, Becca and her mum went along to Lena's house early to help get things ready.

"Do you know everyone who comes here, Lena?" Becca asked, as she helped her make a salad.

"People come and go all the time," Lena said, "but I try to make friends with everyone."

Yes, Becca thought, *Lena's always in and out of everyone's houses.* She seemed to want to know everyone's business. Mum said she was interested in people but Becca thought she was just nosy.

A few hours later, Becca's heart sank when the Millar sisters arrived, with their smug smiles and braying laughs. She was sure neither of *them* was the writer of the diary, as they hated the rocky bay and spent all their time swimming and playing on the sandy beach on the other side, annoying everyone.

Worse still, they were heading straight towards her.

"Why don't you come to the beach with us tomorrow?" Debbie Millar asked, after her mother had given her a warning glance. It was very clear Debbie had been forced to invite Becca to join them.

"Yes, why don't you?" her sister Emma added. "*We* always have lots of fun."

Becca had gone with them once last year and watched in horror as they had run along the beach, kicking sand on everyone as they lay sunbathing, leaping over blankets laid out with picnic food, knocking over cups, bottles and plates of sandwiches. Becca had run behind them, so busy apologizing for them that she hadn't been looking where she was going; she'd crashed into a stand of deckchairs and broken her arm. That was the first of her 'accidents' last year. She wasn't risking *that* again.

"No, thank you," Becca replied. The sisters' grins widened and relief flooded their faces.

"Oh good," Debbie sniggered, and they skipped off, leaving her in peace.

There were a few people at the barbecue who Becca recognized but lots she'd never met before. *Will any of them know anything about the diary?*

She spotted a boy slightly away from the crowds; he didn't seem to know many people either.

"That's Peter," Lena told Becca when she asked. "He's very quiet, too. Why don't you go and talk to him?"

Becca didn't get the chance, though. As soon as he saw her walking towards him he skulked off quickly to play with a ball.

Could he be the writer of the diary? She tried to imagine him hidden in the rocks, scribbling. She was so focused on him she didn't see the shadow looming beside her.

It was Mr Tavish. He'd appeared as if out of nowhere. Strange that she hadn't noticed him earlier; and actually, Lena said he hadn't been invited. So why was he here?

"Are you having fun, Becca?" he asked.

She only nodded. For a second, she almost told him about the diary: she was so desperate to find answers to the questions swimming around in her head. She thought he might know who it belonged to. But something stopped her asking; something she couldn't explain.

Chapter 4

That night there were no nightmares. Becca
was sure it was because she was always
happy here, by the sea, but maybe it was also
because of the diary. She'd been thinking
about it as she drifted off to sleep and it was
the first thing she thought about when she
woke up. In a way, it was like having a secret
friend – someone no one else knew about.
Could the diary belong to Peter? Yesterday,
she had promised herself she'd never read
it again, but it intrigued her. *What kind of
mystery has this boy discovered?*
Assuming the writer *was* Peter.

The diary would have gone by now,
for sure. Even if it didn't belong to Peter,
someone would have found and moved it by
now. *I'll go and check anyway, as soon as I can
get away*, she thought.

Lena dropped in that morning just as Becca was leaving. "Off on your own again, Becca?" she asked. "Where do you go all day?"

"Just down to the rocks," Becca replied, wondering why she seemed so interested.

Lena turned to her mum. "I think she'd be safer on the sandy side of the bay – much safer."

Becca held her breath, waiting for her mother to agree with her friend. But she didn't.

"Becca never goes far, Lena. She'll be fine."

First, Mr Tavish had warned her to be careful and now Lena was telling her where she'd be safe. *Why does everyone want to wrap me in cotton wool?* brooded Becca.

As soon as she reached her secret place, her mood changed. The diary was there, exactly where she'd left it, tucked tight in the little cranny between the rocks. *Maybe the writer isn't around any more. If so, it can't be Peter*, she pondered.

Becca pulled out the plastic bag and tucked herself between the rocks. She slipped out the diary and began to read.

Wednesday 10th July

The boat is back but this time I saw it sailing into the bay, which is strange. Boats never come here - it's too shallow and rocky - but this little boat sailed right in and the men on deck hoisted a red flag.

Why did they do that? Is it a signal of some kind?

Becca stood up and looked out to sea. She gasped. There, anchored in the bay, was a boat with a red flag fluttering in the breeze. *Could it be the same boat the author of the diary had seen? They were right, boats never came into this bay. So why had this one?*

Becca was just about to sit down and open the diary again when she saw someone coming. It was Peter, the boy from the barbecue. *It is his diary after all! Has to be.* Becca fumbled, pushing it into the plastic bag, returning it exactly as she had found it before he came any closer. Then she leapt out of her place in the rocks so suddenly he jumped back.

"Where were you hiding?" he asked.

"I wasn't hiding," Becca said, too quickly. She was sure she looked guilty. She blushed. "I always come here. Do you?"

"Sometimes," he said gruffly. "Although it's not as pretty on this side. Too many rocks."

"I like rocks," she said, defensively. *Why do I sound so guilty?*

He looked at her strangely but said nothing. Becca didn't know what to say so she scurried past him, back up the beach. She didn't stop until she reached her garden. Turning round, she saw Peter down by the shore, skimming stones across the water. *Is he watching the boat with its red flag too? Or, is he waiting for me to leave so he can be alone to write in his diary once again?*

Chapter 5

The nightmares returned that night. Only this time there was no monster: it was just a seagull, pecking and pulling at her hair and her clothes while she tried to shield herself with her hands. She'd been running but had found a safe place in the rocks when, all at once, the seagull had soared above her. Only now it wasn't after Becca: it was after the diary, plucking at the crack in the rocks until it pulled the plastic bag free. She awoke just as more seagulls descended, tearing at it with their beaks.

The diary. It was all she seemed to think about. *Why is it so important to me?*

"How would you like to spend the day in town with me?" her mum asked at breakfast, interrupting Becca's thoughts.

"I thought you were going with Lena?"

"She's not feeling too well today. Terrible migraine. Anyway, I'd much rather spend the day with you."

Becca was sure it was a lie. Her mum was worried about her, concerned that she spent too much time on her own, always scared she was going to have one of her 'accidents'. But Becca desperately wanted to go back to the bay to see if the boat was still there and, more importantly, to read more of the diary.

Her mum stared at Becca, still waiting for her answer.

"I'd love to go, Mum," Becca said at last.

While Becca waited outside for her mum, she saw the Millar sisters coming towards the house. They were the *last* people she wanted to see so she hid behind the garden wall. As they drew closer, she could hear them talking about her.

"Mum says we've got to ask her to come to the beach with us again." It was Debbie who said it and she didn't sound at all happy.

There was a loud tut. "We *did* ask her and she said no!" Emma replied. "She's so boring and scared of everything. No wonder she hasn't got any friends – such a scaredy-cat."

Becca sank back against the wall. She didn't want to hear any more. Was she boring? Was she scared of everything? Even a silly nightmare frightened her.

I wish I could be different, she thought. *I wish, just once, I could be brave.*

Chapter 6

For the whole day, all Becca could think about were the diary, the boat and the mysterious red flag. It was almost dark before they got home and there was a storm coming. *No chance of heading to the rocks tonight*, she grumbled to herself.

Becca hardly slept that night. She was afraid of the monsters waiting for her in her dreams and, besides, her mind was too full for sleep. She sat in bed listening to the wind and imagining the boat tossing and turning on the stormy sea.

She was up before her mum the next day.

"You're an early bird," Mum said, when she found Becca already eating her cereal at the kitchen table. "Did you sleep well?" Her mum tried to hide her concern about the nightmares – she knew Becca thought she was fussing but she couldn't help worrying.

"Slept like a log," Becca lied, then she added. "Why do they say that? Slept like a log? Logs can't sleep, can they?"

Mum shrugged. "I suppose it's because logs just lie still, the way you do when you have a good night's sleep." Then she laughed. "Trust you to ask that, Becca. You're so curious. You always have been, about everything."

That's true. Always curious but timid. She remembered what the Millar sisters had called her. *Scaredy-cat.*

"Are you going to the beach with the girls?" her mum asked.

Becca didn't want to lie but she didn't want to tell the truth either.

"Maybe later," she said. *That's almost the truth, isn't it?*

Becca hurried off after breakfast, promising her mum she'd be careful. Almost immediately she collided with Lena: she'd appeared out of nowhere. Becca stumbled backwards.

"What were you saying about being careful?" Lena laughed and helped her up. "I think you really *should* stay away from the rocks, Becca."

Another warning, Becca thought.

Mum said. "She's going to the beach with the Millar girls."

"Rather you than me," Lena said softly, and Becca managed a smile.

"Don't go too far," Mum called, and Lena turned to Becca and smiled. "That's one thing you don't have to worry about with Becca. She always does as she's told. Don't you, Becca?"

It sounded like an insult: no one ever had to worry about her, she always did as she was told, she never did anything wrong. Becca began to run.

Scaredy-cat.

She could almost hear the Millar sisters shout after her. She slipped on the wet rocks and that made her even angrier. She was boring and timid and accident-prone!

Becca looked out at the bay – the boat was gone. *Of course it's gone!* she thought and hurried to her spot. She desperately felt for the plastic bag. It was still where she'd left it the other day. She took the diary out of the bag, opened it and began to read again.

This morning the boat is gone.
I saw it go. I watched them
carrying something off it: heavy
wooden crates with strange holes
pierced in them. They waded
towards the shore with them in
their arms - boxes of all different
sizes. Then I watched them
loading the boxes into a van and
then drive off. Two of the men
returned to the boat. I think
they're smugglers. I should tell
Mr Tavish but I see him watching
me and someone here has to be
helping them - maybe it's him.
I don't think I can trust him.
No, I won't tell him. I won't tell
anyone, not yet. First I have to
find out what's in those boxes.

Chapter 7

Becca snapped the diary shut. *This is all made up! It's written by someone inventing an adventure for themself, telling lies, and I'm falling for it. Smuggling!* She almost threw the diary as far as she could into the sea.

But she didn't. It wasn't her book. It belonged to someone else and she shouldn't even be reading it.

She sighed. Here she was, doing the right thing again.

She put the diary back and ran home. This time she really was finished with it. She wouldn't look at it again.

But it seemed the diary wasn't finished with her. All that day, she couldn't stop thinking about it. It was as if it was calling to her, wanting her to read on, and she knew she couldn't resist.

It was late afternoon when Becca went back to the rocks but she'd made a promise to herself. She would read the diary one more time. Then, she really would forget about it. If she wanted to read fiction, she'd buy a novel.

Thursday 18th July

It's back. The boat. I'm looking at it right now as I write. The red flag is up: the signal that they're ready. Tonight, I'm going to come back down here and watch. I'm going to find out exactly what is in those boxes and when I write again, the mystery will be solved. I'm determined to find out the truth.

Becca flicked quickly to the next page and the next. There was nothing. Every page was blank.

Why? Had they grown bored with the diary? Had the weather improved and they'd forgotten all about the mystery?

Or ... was the story true? Had they sneaked down to the shore that very night? Had they finally discovered what was in those boxes? Had something happened to them, something so terrible they were never able to come back for the diary?

She could never be that brave: to go down to the shore in the dark, alone.

Scaredy-cat.

The words seemed to be almost whispered to her on the breeze.

Scaredy-cat.

Maybe it was all a made-up story in someone's wild imagination – but Becca had seen that boat too and the red flag. She knew that boats never came into this bay because it was rocky and dangerous … but it was also secluded. No one could see what went on here.

Except curious people, like the author of the diary, or Becca.

The author hadn't come back, though. Becca felt as if she knew them now; she knew that they were brave and that something must have happened that prevented them from coming back for their diary. Something bad.

Becca stood up and looked out over the bay.

The boat was back.

Chapter 8

The red flag was flying. As soon as Becca saw it she made her decision. She didn't care how silly it sounded – she was going out tonight to finish what the author of the diary had started. The boat might be gone tomorrow so tonight could be her last chance to find out what was happening.

Maybe nothing.

Or, perhaps she would see the men unloading boxes as they had done before and, if they did, she was going to find out what was in them.

Becca had never felt so determined. She would come back to the beach tonight, even it meant sneaking out of her house. If she didn't, she felt as if she'd be letting the diary-writer down.

Becca couldn't eat a thing at dinner; pushing her food around her plate with her fork. Her stomach was churning.

"Are you okay, Becca?"

She knew her cheeks flushed when her mum asked her that. For a moment, she wondered if she could tell her mum about the diary ... but she knew what she would say: that it was nonsense, not real. Then she would forbid her from ever going down to the rocks again.

"Are you enjoying your holiday?" Mum was speaking again but before Becca could answer she said, "I wish you weren't always so alone."

"Honest, Mum. I'm having a great time."

It was true. The mystery was exhilarating. Even if it turned out to be nothing at all, it was thrilling. Yet something was telling her, it *wasn't* nothing.

"Is Lena coming over tonight?" Becca asked. She was hoping Lena wasn't, as her mum would go to bed earlier then; Becca was desperate to leave as soon as possible.

"No, she's got one of her migraines again."

Becca waited until Mum was asleep before she slipped out of the house.

It was a clear night. A crescent moon hung in a starlit sky. *Will that be a good or bad thing?* she wondered. She'd have to be careful she wasn't spotted. She'd taken precautions and dressed head to toe in black: her jeans, her hooded sweater, all black. She'd done everything she could to camouflage herself. *Have they done the same?* She also had her phone with her – at the first sign of danger she'd call the police.

When Becca reached the rocks, she crouched down and began to crawl between them. There, hidden out of sight, she could secretly watch the boat, bobbing close to the shore. It was camouflaged too, a dark boat against a pitch-black sea. She could see two figures loading boxes from the boat into a rowing boat tied up beside it. Becca crept closer. The rowing boat pushed off towards the shore. As the boat neared the stony shore, the figure on board leapt into the shallow water and began hauling it on to the beach.

Another hooded figure, waiting on the beach, ran forward to help and together they began lifting boxes of all sizes from the boat, one by one.

Becca was hardly breathing as she watched it all. She was afraid but there was more than fear churning inside her. There was something else, a feeling she couldn't explain.

The figures were now lifting the biggest of the boxes out of the rowing boat. *It looks different somehow. Not a box – is it a crate? Just as the author of the diary had seen?*

The shadowy figures laid the crate on the beach and began carrying one of the other boxes up to a van parked further up the shingle. Becca could just make out the back doors lying open. She had to see what was in those boxes near the sea edge. While their backs were turned, this was her chance. She began crawling across the shingle on her belly the way she'd seen spies do in films.

She was almost there. The figures hadn't even reached the van yet, which meant she still had time to get to the boxes before they came back. She crawled closer, trying to imagine what might be inside that largest crate. *Something heavy for sure,* she thought, *as they really struggled to lift it out of the boat. Gold bars perhaps?*

She was only a short distance away when she froze, unable to move, because now she could see it wasn't a box at all. Or a crate.

It was a cage.

And something was moving inside it.

Chapter 9

Two green slits of eyes turned to her. She
couldn't breathe as the monster from her
nightmares stared at her. Becca scrambled
back. She had to get away. She couldn't
understand how this could be happening.
Her mind was in a whirl ... and all the time
those piercing eyes watched her. Suddenly,
a tail flicked and the eyes blinked just once.
Becca gasped.

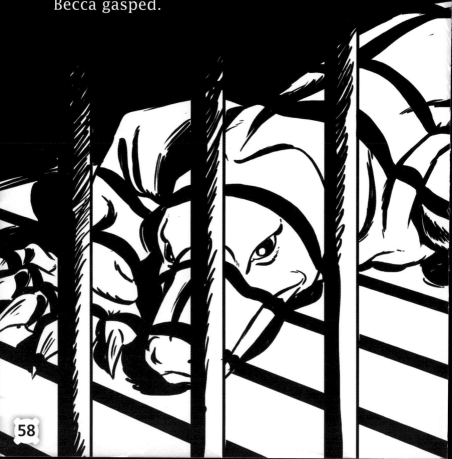

Any moment now, the monster will rush from the cage and chase me, just like before. Last time the cage had been open.

Last time?

What did she mean, last time?

Something was inching its way into her memory, like a door in a dark room slowly being opened.

The tail flicked again. The eyes blinked. Now she could make out spines running down its back. The mouth opened and she saw its sharp teeth glint in the moonlight. She forced herself to stare back.

She had run last time.

Last time?

What did she mean? Had she been here before on this moonlit beach? Had she seen this monster before?

Suddenly, the door in her mind was flung wide open and it all came flooding back to her. The boat sailing into the bay, the red flag being hoisted: she had seen it all. She had come here to investigate, had seen the monster and the open cage, and had been so afraid it would chase her she had run and run; and then somewhere high on the rocks she had tumbled and hit her head. That was the last thing she remembered. When she had opened her eyes, she was on the beach, alone. It was dawn and the boat was gone; and so was the monster ... and so was her memory.

Now Becca remembered everything.

There had never been anyone else.

She was the author of the diary.

Chapter 10

Everything was suddenly clear. She had written the diary and hidden it away. She hadn't recognized the handwriting because her right arm had been in plaster after her collision with the deckchairs and she'd used her left hand to write. She looked again at the cage and she smiled.

It wasn't a monster at all.

It was a large lizard. Now those slits of eyes didn't look scary at all – the poor thing just looked scared.

Becca moved closer and peered at the next cage. There was another lizard, not as big as the first but just as strange-looking. *Are they smuggling these strange creatures? Do people do that?*

She would have to get off this beach and warn the police. She glanced towards the van. One of the figures was still there, still unaware of her presence. The other was probably inside the van. Becca stood up. She got out her phone. No reception. She would have to make a run for home. However, she only got a few steps before a hand grabbed her shoulder.

"I thought it was you."

Becca swung round. She knew that voice. "Lena, thank goodness ... we have to hurry. We have to call the police." Everything came babbling out, about the boat and the lizard. She was no longer alone – Lena was here. "I think they're smugglers ..." Becca stopped as a thought struck her. "I thought you had a migraine ..."

Becca said no more. It was as if there was a jigsaw tumbling about in her mind. Lena was dressed all in black, just like the figure she had seen waiting on the beach, and she always seemed to have a migraine when the boat came in. In that moment, all the pieces of the jigsaw clicked into place.

Lena was one of them.

"I did keep warning you, Becca, to stay away from these rocks," Lena said, coldly.

"I don't *always* do what I'm told though, do I?" Becca said, glad that her voice sounded firm and unafraid.

"Just what do I do with you now, though? You've 'seen too much' as they say," said Lena.

A chill cut through Becca. *I've seen too much? Surely they don't intend to …? An accident in the water … 'Accident-prone little Becca, all her own fault … slipping on the rocks. Again.'*

NO!

Becca gave Lena a push. It took Lena so much by surprise that it sent her sprawling down on to the shingle. Becca began to run but Lena was on her feet in an instant.

Becca glanced behind her but as she did so her foot slipped and she stumbled. She was never going to make it to the road.

Then she remembered her secret place. If she could make it there, she'd be hidden from view; and dressed all in black, in the dark, there was a chance Lena wouldn't see her at all. Becca darted between the rocks, crouching low, trying to melt into the shadows.

Becca heard Lena's angry voice somewhere behind her.

"You little so-and-so. You're going to be very sorry about this."

But Becca was already safely tucked away in her secret place. All she needed to do now was ring the police – if she could. She pulled out her phone. Two bars of reception. *Great, it's working.* Steadying her shaking hands, she was beginning to type in the numbers when a voice rang out above her.

"You won't need that, Becca."

She looked up and saw the ashen face of Mr Tavish looming above her.

Chapter 11

Becca was ready to scream but then, to her surprise, Mr Tavish smiled a big, wide, friendly smile.

"Are you okay, Becca?" he asked warmly.

She couldn't speak.

He wasn't alone: police were swarming all over the rocks and beach. One of them grabbed Lena's hands and handcuffed them behind her back. Becca could see that the other black-clad figures were being rounded up and arrested too.

At last she found her voice. "Mr Tavish?" Becca was amazed. She'd been so sure he was one of the other figures on the beach. "Are you a police officer?"

"I used to be. I knew there was something fishy going on so I've had my eye on Lena for a while. People were coming here on holiday and then leaving in the middle of the night, as if they had something to hide, and it all led back to her. Isn't that right, Lena?"

"Do you know how much people will pay for these animals?" Lena snapped. "Just to be able to say they have something no one else has. They were going to buy them from *someone*. Why not me?" Her voice was bitter. "We weren't hurting anyone."

"But they're endangered!" said Becca, horrified.

"And it's not just lizards," Mr Tavish said, "but any rare and endangered species. It's a very lucrative business." He looked at Lena. "If it isn't stopped, there won't be any of these creatures left in the wild."

When the police had taken Lena and her fellow smugglers away, Mr Tavish turned to Becca.

"You're clever, Becca, and brave, coming down here in the middle of the night. But you're going to have to be even braver now … and face your mum!"

"Does she know I'm here? Is she really mad at me?" Becca asked, worry creeping into her voice.

He smiled. "I think she'll relent when she hears how you've helped catch a band of international smugglers."

"I did, didn't I?"

Becca grinned – she couldn't help it. *Just wait until I tell the Millar sisters about this!*

Find out more ...

For another Who Dunnit? story read *The Snatcher*.

Solve a mystery with Inspector Textor in *A Super Sleuth's Manual*.

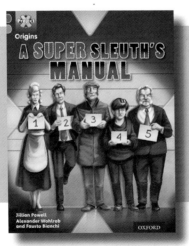